About Her

An Anthology of Poems

I0654283

Navpreet Saini

Sahityapedia Publishing

Sahityapedia Publishing

Noida (India) - 201301

Telephone - (+91) -9618066119

Email - publish@sahityapedia.com

Website - publish.sahityapedia.com

First Edition - 2019

ISBN - 978-93-89100-17-4

Introduction

People say age is just a number and yes that's true, only thing that matters is one's heart. One's heart is filled with many emotions joy, happiness, sorrow and pain. This book covers all these genres and is mainly based on her point of view.

About her tells us how one fell, first heartbreak, how maturity hits and actually pricks, how friends and lovers grow apart with time and how a cheerful heart matures to be rock solid and ice cold.

This book is just a collection of many different poetries, each telling different story of different time. Technically it's all about heartache she experiences not merely of her own but also whatever she gathers from around, which helps her to grow even more. It's more like I say, "MORE THAN LEARNING FROM THEIR MISTAKES, LEARN FROM THEIR PAIN".

Contents

Rising From The Ash

She wished to conquer the world with a smile and loved one on her side........and this way a story began

Rejected by everyone,

Deceived by own loved ones,

Wrapped in lonliness,

She started residing in the darkness.

Kissed by fire, covered by revenge,

Can do anything to avenge....

Rising from ash, she only vowed to thrash.

And this way an innocent one who once decieved, rose from ash - Promised to make them kiss their ass.

My Knight

Only light in the dark,

My knight in the armour,

Though has glittery eyes,

It's only for me that they spark.

Devilish by looks,

For only me he acts like the open book.

Never once acknowledged his own mistake,

It's only for me, for the first time, he actually takes the blame.

Believed to be the most impatient man till the grave, how cute, for me, he actually learns to wait.

Known to be the most matured man walking on the ground,

How can he act such a child when I am around.

Maybe for his nature or his possessive grounds, let me tell you I miss him always but I love him more when he is not around.

Betrayal

She trusted her with her heart,

And she made it clear, to break, it isn't that hard.

Her 15 years of friendship comes as a lie, just for someone else sake, was it really that easy for her to say bye?

Remembering past 15 years, her every memory revolves around, it can be happy, it can be sad she always surround,

for a shattered soul, she comes as a ray of hope, to handle her fears, her insecurities, she was always around.

Sometimes she wonder, is it that easy for her to leave, maybe she wanted to stay, maybe she was waiting for her to say.

New faces, new places, new college but they were the same, she knew, compare to others she was lame, could it be a reason?

The moment they parted ways, on that instant something inside her fades away.

It can be trust, it can be pain but from that day she never felt anything in any way.

Maybe for some spotlight, maybe for some fame or maybe it was really her mistake, otherwise she might had stayed.

Life is a merry go round,
it goes up, it comes
down...teaches you to let go
things which will be rarely
going to come around....

Broken Promise

The trust I broke, the secret I told vanished my all rays of hope,

the pain I give and reason above all,

it doesn't matter anymore,

the damage I did and those broken wings,

still haunt my soul,

although the reason was pure,

but it damaged her whole.

I wished I would have kept that secret which was never mine to told.

One Who Is Holding On.....

To the one who is still holding on

I may had lost myself unlimited times a day,

But you always find a way<THANKS FOR HOLDING ON>

I had cursed myself many times a day,

But you always fetch me out, trying every possible way.<I AM GRATEFUL, YOU DON'T MOVE ON>

I had started to live in the lonliness, I had started to love the darkness.

But you are the one making me realise, how wonder is the light, you are the one making me believe it's the rage, from which I should hide.

I had even cursed you many times, but after everything still seeing you beside, make me believe everything is going to fine.

<THANKS FOR BEING A PERSON TO UNDERSTAND MY SILENCE><THANKS FOR HOLDING ON>

She

She has brightest smile, which can make even sun shine more bright, so I always wonder why she always choose to hide.

She has glow in her eyes but what's strange is she appears to be burning from inside.

She has weird type of calmness in her attitude, same as before the tornado arise.

Appears to be happily ever but something is hidden? Is she broken from inside?

She enjoys the darkness but what's most feard thing is, She is afraid of daylight.

Only thing I know is she is mystery, pure but fragile.

Maturity

Growing day by day, from infant to child, some part of me left away.

Scared, coward and shy learns to survive in every possible way.

Confidence, arrogance and beauty, she adopts all ways.

Living in a cruel world, she never believed in fairytale..

Scared to love, make friends, she decides to write her own tale.

Maintaining distance, keeping secrets, she believed she can live in her own way..

From loving someone to stone hearted, she changed in all ways.

Then something happened, She met someone and guess what that's all it takes, she changed.

Still scared to trust but this time she wanted to believe in fairytale..

Now lets see what will come in this new way.

Herself

She crowned herself.

ditching her fear.

She empowered herself,

facing their hatred.

She conquered her beliefs,

overcoming her superstitions.

She risen above her pain,

fading it away.

She won her own heart,

rejecting fame.

and finally she finds her peace,

by letting everything go away.

Freedom is the state of
mind...
just like after effects of
wine....
It's the peace of one's own
mind....
it's that thirst which only
you can satisfy otherwise
may cost you your entire
life....

Something More

There was a time, she was fat..

There was her, once the baby cat..

There was time and there were them,

Taunts and humiliation but no one to stop them.

There was time she believed in friends..

There was a time she learned innocence is just a trend.

There was a time, she believed beauty and beast can coexist..

There was a time she learned, in this world beast dare not to exist.

Then comes a time she was drawn towards beauty.

And forgets about beast, atlast earns the beauty but lost the inner peace...

Now time has come, she is hot as hell.

Now there was her, once the babycat nows a ladybat..

Now her time has come, now there are few of them..

More of taunts, more of humiliation but now it was something more of her vs something less of them

You Are My Star In Sky

You are that star in sky...so high...

which was not touched.....

but captured by everyone's eye...

You are that star in sky...

Believed to grant any wish...

But only few knows you are so selfish.....

You are that star in sky...when fell...

Never touched the ground..

Still carrying the wishes of everyone around...

You are that star in sky....so sparkling..

That trickles with the time

So self obssess...

Believe to fade moon even if it means to sublime....

You are that star in sky... who helps the lost to be found...

Yet it's always difficult to choose either to follow or turn around...

And yes you are that star in sky....which never touched the ground...

But one day will... suffering same fate...it will left with nothing just dust around

Stranger

It's weird I met a stranger that doesn't appear to me like one.

It's first time I forget about my shy look and talked like a open book.

It's first time I believe I found peace,

It's first time I let my security breach.

The big smile on his face and fear in his eyes,

He came to talk with little courage, that I guess he instantly binds.

I said I don't rememeber much, but he said he remembered me from a class, so please don't misjudge.

I hardly remembered his face but, remembered his name and he hardly knows my name but remembered my face.

It's been 2 years since we met, still he knows everything about me like it's still fresh.

He knows about my curly hairs, he knows about my favourite books, how is it possible i mean I hardly even remember his looks.

Most weird fact is that I never allowed myself to talk to a stranger and now we just exchanged number like it's as easy as chewing wringler.

I think I wanted to check his guts,

So I provide him a chance to text, which i believe with that story he gets.

Slowly, slowly hi, hello turns to never ending chats and my prince charming imagination turns into facts.

His every message makes me blush,

his message make me smile which I never ever have in while....

His every text has something sweet, not flirty, not vulgar

but it gives me peace and that is when I realise he is perfect.

He

His eyes has something unsual, has a spark which lit the flame.

His lame smile compliments the flame.

His eyes symbolise the purity while his smile defines the innocence.

His way of speaking is sweeter than honey, his words can be life threating for anybody.

His height defines his personality while his looks complement him with royalty.

His overall appearence symbolise the perfection but still has something demonic inside his reflection.

Ocean is everything i want
it to be....
Joyfull shores, calming
waves and mysterious
depths....

First Day In College

His first day in college, believe me, his eyes
were the first thing that caught my attention.

It's first thing for me that I wanted to keep
confidential.

Once I believed all boys are same but it's only
him who made me realise that I actually
mistook.

Fighting for seats, for his better view, it felt like
there were just we two.

His way of asking me notes, gives me unlimited
hope, I mean he can ask his new friends why
me, we haven't yet talked.

And one day, he actually called me by my name
and it was first time, I realised I can never be
the same, first time I believe background music
do exist, first time I believe there was really a
feeling in my entire life that I missed.

Waiting

I was waiting for you on the same road where you promised to never let go.

I was waiting for you, sitting on side, where we promised to watch the sunrise.

I had waited for you to come and hug me like never before.

You promised to let me follow wherever you go.

You promised to always choose me before.

Yet you decided to go alone.

Well let's say, this time it's new, you are chosen but I am not.

But wait for me, let's tell god, we both will be chosen or god has to go alone.

Rainy

Those days it rained alot,

she cried from the core.

Wipped her tears so that no one can knew about her fears.

Every morning she woke up with the brightest smile,

Every night only her pillows knew how cloudy its inside.

Her diary screamed about her pain,

It's every page has his name.

He was her passion, she was his game.

He played very well, left in peace but broke her into pieces.

From that day it started to rain, and that's when she learnt to cry from the core.

Miss

I miss those walks.

I miss those you and me talks.

I miss those long nights on phone.

I miss those forever promises that are long gone.

I miss our sarcasm.

I miss those laughs that ends up getting us spasm.

I miss our fights that ends us together.

I miss our moods that even ends up changing the weather.

I miss the old relationship that has changed to core.

I miss the US that left you and me to go.

Well I miss because I hold on.

And with ending this I promise I am moving on.

Once In A Blue Moon

Like once in a blue moon,

with his pictures, his memories again storm in
my room,

but this time it's something new,

stuck there for a moment,

more they grew,

shocked for a while,

felt like paralysed,

in each part of my mind they groove.

 Tears in my eyes,

I was back on square one from distance that I
travelled miles,

dared to tear,

this time I place it near,

there was a flood of memories that arise and
there was still that smile with which I again
prayed for his smile, forgetting his lies.

Only in darkness, you will
know the importance of the
light, only in moment of
need, you will know, you
are the light.

Eyes

There is something different, something strange, something weird, I don't know but there is something in his eyes.

I wonder is it really a mystery to read what's inside.

Those are so big, magnificient and white.

No one can believe they can hide something so wild.

No anger, no love neither madness nor the lonlines, how can they appear so empty, so neutral everytime.

Those eyes always appear so understanding wanted to be read,

so indulging yet they can diverge anyone to mislead.

Those are so deep to drown yet practically, they are like horizon.

They are so pure, so transparent, so indulging but still has something inside them which is diverging.

Those eyes definately have something that has to be discovered which is yet undercover.

Those eyes have something, something strange, something different that I wanted to read but I couldn't in any way.

His Secret

Only he knew she was the unforgettable
chapter of his life,

deepest secret which worth the fight.

He neither confess nor forgets, there was a pain
that he hides.

she still lives in his soul, though they were the
opposite poles.

His demons wanted to evolve but she was the
only one for whom he learnt to control.

Confuse

Her eyes has weird type of shyness... tired of waiting to be read...desperate to say something....at the same time so cold left him wondering that what is it?

Her lips always opens to say something but stops in mid....acting like freak...maybe scared....maybe desperate....even sometimes mean....

Her gestures always have given a mixed signals....trembled from near....bold from here...

Sometimes tries to formal....sometimes being normal...always left him wondering why is it or something wrong with him?

Convinced

Though she is convincing herself that he may love her the most,

His ignorance is enough to realise she is wrong.

Now she is really convinced they can never live along,

So she finds a way to move on.

When she is convinced she has moved on,

His single stare is enough to made her realise she is back on.

Though she is convinced that she can never ever be jealous,

But his way of staring others is enough to make her envious.

Though she knows he is a stud, flirt and total fraud,

Still she believes his eyes which are enough to cover up his lies.

Though she is convinced friendship is way more important than love,

But everytime he stare her friend, there is a
destructive thought that fails to suppress.

Though she was convinced she hate him from
the core,

But everytime she forgets there is a part of him
that still lives within her soul.

Misery

She has started believing misery is her fate,

She has started to close all the open gates.

Her trembling belief tells us her story.

First thing she learns, there is no such word as sorry.

Care is second thing she is scared off,

irony is love still comes first, life is like just****off.

Her shattered dreams, screams about her pain,

Only her diary knows whom to blame.

Only thing she learns love only snatches from you,

it's the hate that catches for you.

Everything she learns costs her a bit,

but the total process costs her innocence and

maturity hits her with the brick.

Broken from inside but
darling she is even lethal
from outside...beware

Me

I wanted to find me, new me, stronger me, and in search of this me, I have already lost the orignal me.

Now

I always have smile on my face but I wonder if it shows what my heart really consolidates.

People say they have never seen me cry but who knows how many tears I have shed for my eyes to look that much dry.

People say they love my charm but I wonder if they will ever know, to compensate I have lost all my warmth.

My friends love my positive attitute but I always wonder if they will ever know how much negativity actually contributes.

People that surrounds me, call me bold and cute but how much they knew, not enough to know about my solitude.

People that I once call mine are history and people that call me theirs are new, And I believe history repeats itself so I always consider to flew, even if the case will be once in blue moon.

Though people are new but better than my old crew.

And though I have lost myself but now I am modified not to walk but to flew.

More Warm Or Harm

She has found something, since then she has adapted it well and now I wonder is she turned hopeless?

Her newly found strange calmness pricks me hard,

Her newly found weird patience bleeds my heart,

Her changed attitude is enough to keep her warm,

Her newly found forgiving nature, but then I wonder if there was any harm?

Her lack of interest, no hopes, never ending smile, lost expectations and newly found artificial charm.

But may be good, granted with something new, valuable enough to keep her warm.

Her newly found peace, her symbol of victory, ravishing glory, no emotions and fake charm...now I wonder if it can cause any more harm?

Emptiness

She has something which can never be expressed.

Maybe it's not serious but she has some sort of emptiness.

Otherwise how can she feel alone even in her own home.

How can she don't feel any emotion among the people which are her own.

Sometimes I wonder how talented she is, she learnt to fake a smile.

It's amazing that she haven't felt anything in a while,

It's mystery how she manage to convince everyone that these emotions are her own,

Despite the fact maybe she is deattaching from all.

Maybe it's to late to discuss, maybe she has already deattached from every single one of us.

Maybe it's crazy, maybe it's insane but ask her what's the real pain.

Good Enough To Be True

She is keen, her eyes are pythons green.

Her face has a charismatic glow, she always goes with the flow.

Her speech screams a different accent, she has a flowery scent.

Good enough to be true,

let's start with reality check and ofcourse how can I forget she is somewhat tomato head.

Her day start by swaring*******, but my god she is so caring.

Her punjabi is so cute but she hates those Indian suits.

She looks like an innocent book but believe me she has devlish mind but MY GOD HELL PRETTY by looks.

She can die for friends but let me remind you before showing your confidence just clean your lens.

At last, to be clear, she is good enough to be true but bad enough to make you two.

Light your darkness with
your fire

She

Fire in her eyes,

Storm residing inside,

can kill anyone with her eyes,

still gives a new life with a smile,

has a glow on her face which compliments her flame,

everything in front of her looks lame,

has a stone cold heart,

keeping her warm but there is no one to cherish her charm.

LPU

Ballooned face left home, scared and shy moveforth.

Wearing a mask with big smile, confidence and proudy indian entered the college henceforth.

No hopes, no expectations, just for parents sake entered the class.

With few Indians, Zambians, Africans and Arabians I was dumped in a class.

Just need sake friends, left many memories that I can't forget.

One was helper, one was performer, one was navigator and so many gossipers, I regret there was a family that I left.

Zambians were perfect friends, Arabians and Muslims were perfect defination of cuteness, Indians were as usual perfect irritators.

<MEMORIES>want to made many more but left with few. Still all are in touch that's why I know how unfortunate I am that I left.

Memories are still fresh that's why I know it's
not easy to forget.

Feelings

She always knew but she never admit, She always cared but she never showed, she always feard but never said.

After several years, she knows she still cares . She still feels the same butterflies.

His wink can still make her day, for his single glimpse, She still bunk her day.

Until now she still maintained her habit to see him every single day . She still feels like dying when she fails to maintain.

His ignorance still affects her but she's not gonna say . She still believes every action has equal and opposite reaction . She believes may be one day he will say.

But her hopes are falling still she wishes to stay . She knows she loves him but how can she stay, till now he don't even say.

well it also doesn't suit his playboy look to say . But even if he does how can she stay?

After so many years does he means whatever he says?

Eye Contact

Something is happening since then,

Just 2second eye contact leaves so much loose ends.

They started to wonder is it spark or it's the intensity that troubles them...

They both knew they felt it, one wanted to explore,

other choose to ignore,

knowingly one still fell even more

and believe her, deep down it grows,

It's not the first time she fell but this she just floats,

though he wanted to worship the loyalty, wanted to one women's guy, wanted to wait for someone special,

still he moves with the flow, and even for him it grows, when he figured to express, when he can no longer suppress, She waited much longer at that instant such that till then she turned hopeless.

Don't hold a grudge, just
hold a bulldozer once for all

Actions

For every smile she fakes,

there is a lie that she made.

For every effort she makes,

his avoidance makes her go insane.

For every step she takes,

he made it go in viens..

Shame

It's shame we are not going to be together
again.

It's shame that as promised we are not going to
end up together in frames.

It's shame everytime our memories will still
bring the same smile on our face.

It's shame that we will be sad and will end up
even getting more mad.

It's shame that it will never going to be same
again.

It's shame even if we will ever get chance, none
of us is going to change...

It's shame our ego's win and we lose to change.

It's shame we are never going to be same.

Believed

Once he had spark in his eyes, now those are ice cold and white.

Once I believed there was innocence residing inside, now I believe those were just tacts to hypnotise.

Once I believed there was a smile making everything fine, now I believe there is a lust hiding inside.

Once I believed his heart was made of gold but now I know it's nothing more than a stone.

I was living in a dream, it just breaks up, and left me alone, just finding a way how to cope all alone.

Lie

Like once in a blue moon,

Mom again stormed in my room, but this time it's something new,

I had to face her wrath,

She wanted to know about that brat,

Brat from my last story and this time she is not going so easy,

I told her it's my imagination but she was firm like she was not ready for any negotiation.

I told her that was just for rhyme but she was confirm there were feelings hiding behind,

She didn't bother to listen anything so I accept the feelings although those were not purely mine,

Though he had no name but there is a imagination which gives me pain,

I described while hearing about someone else pain, its my hobby to take it up although I know there is no gain,

At last she was finally convinced about ideas of
my crazy brain,

That was the time I realise I have done phD in
brain games.

Happiness

Here and there it's happiness that u find everywhere.

It's the peace in your eyes seeing your family after long time.#HOSTLERS

It's a proud feeling that a father gets seeing you sipping life as easy as lime.#FATHER

Its in a sacrifice that your mother makes, keeping you in her womb as long as it takes.#MOTHER

It's in a tom and jerry fight which makes us believe, we are incomplete atleast in this life.#SIBLINGS

It's in game of stealing and sharing with our lifelines..#FAMILY

Admist The Crowd

Admist the crowd, when no one actually surrounds.....

Admist the crowd, when it's only the music that winds me around....

Admist the crowd, it's my consious that I found...

Admist the crowd, it's the genuine peace that I found....

Admist the crowd, only place where I love to be surround..

Admist the crowd, it's the lost me that I found

I believe in karma, but
when i don't find one, i
decide to be the one

Dreams

I don't know how i am saying but can u get away?

haven't shown till now, why u bother to come now.

It's not I never wanted but how can you bring my worst nightmare all along...

From past 20 years you haven't shown, now suddenly, how can he come along..

Each passing day I wanted to fade his memory away,

Please stop trying to bring him back in my life all over again.

He's not in my heart, not in my mind then how can he be wandering in my subconsious mind...

Stop elevating my hopes when u know he can never be mine.

I guess I should stop pretending and fight for what is mine.

Till then I know it's big to ask but can u stop messing with my mind.

Dream Like Life

Cheers to our dream like life,

Now we are together bind.

Cheers to our dream like life,

For our future, love and lies.

Cheers to our dream like life,

Like the sweet and sour wine.

Cheers to our dream like life.

Where balanced yin and yang lies.

Cheers to our dream like life,

Where shadow of our hate and fear are going to balance the stage.

Cheers to our dream like life,

Where we don't need to hide.

Cheers to our dream like life,

Where we will learn to stand together even in tides.

Cheers to our dream like life,

Where we will together grow and can peacefully die.

Cheers to our dream like life,

Now we are forever bind.

Cold

It hurts when no one takes the stand,

am I that much bad?

Maybe I am turning cold but is it that bad to be bold?

I had cried a lot but there was no one to make me stop.

Now I decide to get the payback why should I stop?

I always stand alone in the crowd so I decided why not to feel proud.

Before someone knocked me out, I decide to have some showdown.

Tables turns this time, afraid and scared learns to fight,

She has changed, it can be bad for most but it's undeniably good for her life.

Maybe for good, may be for bad,

She has turned cold but definitely she is no longer sad.

Suicide

Everyone criticised her for her suicide.

Everyone posted quotes that how precious is life.

Everyone shows their concern but where were they when she was alive.

No one had just walked in her shoes and u think she was a fool to end her life.

During her last days, hadn't anyone noticed any change? She was a fighter struggling for her life.

She might had tried to talk with friends, maybe family but where were they, when she wanted to confide.

Maybe those conversations might had worked, maybe those friendly hugs might had worked.

Yes it is not their mistake, maybe that moment she might had lacked that courage but don't you dare confuse her with coward, if you do, first think about walking in those shoes, just remember she was brave enough to live so long.

Even she had some dreams, even she was someone's queen,

So stop these quotes because these are even worse than those lethal attitutes.

Light

It's time for me to get numb...

My inspirations I once had are already being dumped..

My love had been thrown away from my soul...

The friends that I had were already faded with time...

My laughter has been lost..

The road I wanted to take was long gone...

I am lost in my path...

Everyday I wished to be slayed....

I am tired of waiting for the impossible light....

It's getting more and more darker and cold...

My eyes are getting heavy and I believe finally it's time for them to close

Every night follows the dark and every day follows the night, and that's how there is always a chance for the fresh start.

Unspoken

Maybe I failed to confess, consider I am not direct.

But you actually failed to read my tears, Are you really not that weird?

Maybe my mischieves were beyond your imagination, but everytime you react, Are you really a fool or want me to be exact?

Maybe everytime seeing you, my raised voice, you consider, was a prank.

But everytime you flaunt, you were really being that much frank?

Maybe I have taken your actions wrong, but are you really too dumb to know? Even when you were playing along?

Yours

Moving towards you, I guess I have come far away from myself.

I have started to search myself in your eyes.

Hoping to see me there, I guess I am losing my mind

Praying to be a beat of your heart and reason of your smile.

I guess I have to first cover a distance worth a mile.

Scared to tell that I want to live by your side,

I have already forgotten my world and ready to join in yours for my entire life.

I guess I was happy to be a shadow but now I want to give a try, to make you mine.

Grown

As I was learning to grow, more than anything the time flows.

And I learn there are some people I need to let go.

Slowly and steady as the pain started to subside,

Not only me but my emotions also learns to hide.

As I was learning to be strong,

Not only my mind, my heart also turns to be cold.

As I stopped being a believer,

Not only my faith but also my fears tends to dissipiate.

As I decided to go with the flow,

Little did I know I had already grown.

Mom

Simple like flower, elegant like star,

Lovely as chocolate, sexy as hell,

Temper be pepper, still binding us together,

She is different, she is special,

Melt like a candle, strong like stone,

There is no one like her, guess who? She is

MOM

Friends

I REMEMBER

When I fell, the one who rushed was someone new.

When I was wretching in pain, the person who asked my welfare was new

When I was lying on the ground, the people who panicked were all new.

When I was trying to compose myself, the one who asked to pick me up was new.

When I asked for a minute to check my phone, I laughed and the people who joined me, they were all new.

When I fell, the first hand that comes to lift me was not known.

And that's how I found my new family, all of those morons.

New lifes

Let's cheers to our new lifes

For the future that will definetely going to shine

Let's celebrate for moving on this new stage of life

For only we are the one moving forth leaving hundreds behind

Let's celebrate our parents victory who were always there standing on our sides.

Follow our duty to Make them feel proud reaching new heights.

Let's be proud for coming under this outstanding spotlight.

For learning from pros and getting a prestigious opportunity to outshine.

So let's enjoy together coming every moment of life.

Let's grab this opportunity and together reach those heights.

So cheers to our new life,

And together work hard to shine

Congrats

Wishing both of you for entering a new phase of life...

With lots of love, the infinite smiles..

Congratulating both of you moving ahead one more step in this journey of life....

For the future sweet and sour fights...

Praying for both of your happiness which is now together bind...

Sometimes in dark and sometimes in light..

Blessing you with lots of brain, patience and spirit to compromise..

As they will come handy in solving any of those future fights..

And at last but not the least wishing a newly married couple a happily ever after life..

Conclusion

To conclude, emotions are part of us and here I emphasise on sorrow little more than other emotion because it is most noxious among all. Person with sorrow may have a power to arise and shine like never before or may have a power to destructs himself like never before.